Hello, Family Members,

Learning to read is one of the most im
of early childhood. **Hello Reader!** boo
children become skilled readers who
readers learn to read by remembering frequently used words like "the," "is," and "and"; by using phonics skills to decode new words; and by interpreting picture and text clues. These books provide both the stories children enjoy and the structure they need to read fluently and independently. Here are suggestions for helping your child *before*, *during*, and *after* reading:

Before

- Look at the cover and pictures and have your child predict what the story is about.
- Read the story to your child.
- Encourage your child to chime in with familiar words and phrases.
- Echo read with your child by reading a line first and having your child read it after you do.

During

- Have your child think about a word he or she does not recognize right away. Provide hints such as "Let's see if we know the sounds" and "Have we read other words like this one?"
- Encourage your child to use phonics skills to sound out new words.
- Provide the word for your child when more assistance is needed so that he or she does not struggle and the experience of reading with you is a positive one.
- Encourage your child to have fun by reading with a lot of expression . . . like an actor!

After

- Have your child keep lists of interesting and favorite words.
- Encourage your child to read the books over and over again. Have him or her read to brothers, sisters, grandparents, and even teddy bears. Repeated readings develop confidence in young readers.
- Talk about the stories. Ask and answer questions. Share ideas about the funniest and most interesting characters and events in the stories.

I do hope that you and your child enjoy this book.

—Francie Alexander
Reading Specialist,
Scholastic's Instructional Publishing Group

To Melissa
— R.G.G.

To Joe and Tommy
— D.R.

Library of Congress Cataloging-in-Publication Data
Gelman, Rita Golden.
Hello cat, you need a hat / by Rita Golden Gelman; illustrated by Dana Regan.
p. cm.— (Hello reader! Level 2)
Summary: A young girl tries to convince a grumpy cat to wear a variety of hats, including a walkie-talkie hat, a monkey hat, and a cowboy hat.
ISBN 0-439-04021-3
[1. Hats —Fiction. 2. Cats —Fiction. 3. Stories in rhyme.]
I. Regan, Dana, ill. II. Title.
III. Series.
PZ8.3.G2Hc 1998
[E]—dc21 98-27403
CIP
AC

12 11 10 9 8 7 6 5 4 3 2 9/9 0/0 01 02 03 04

Printed in the U.S.A. 24
First printing, December 1998

Hello, Cat, You Need a Hat

by Rita Golden Gelman
Illustrated by Dana Regan

Hello Reader! — Level 2

SCHOLASTIC INC. Cartwheel BOOKS®
New York Toronto London Auckland Sydney

Oh, look.
Just look!
Your head is bare.
I have some hats that you can wear.
Come over here.
I'll give you some.

I do not want one.
Hats are dumb.

I have rain hats . . .

. . . hats for sun.

You'll never catch me
wearing one.

Hats for cold with fur and ear things.

Walkie-talkie hats
that hear things.

Monkey hats for getting money.

Hats with nets for getting honey.

Try *this* hat.
You really should.

If I wanted to,
I would!

Hats to swim in.

Hats to hide in.

Hats to be a groom
and bride in.

You may have *this* hat.
You may.

I do not want it.
Go away!

Bands wear hats.
Police do, too.

Teams wear hats.
So why can't you?

Hats for cowgirls.

Hats for knights.

Hats for welding.

Hats with lights.

Hats with chin things.
Hats with spin things.

Hats they give you when you win things.

I never spin.
I never win.
And I want nothing on my chin.

Hats for crowning.

Hats for clowning.

Hats for cooking.

I’m not looking.

Bat hats.
Mouse hats.
Witch hats, too.

If witches wear them,
WHY CAN'T YOU?

Fire hats are best of all.
The way they make the water fall.

Have one.
Have one of your own.

Get out of here.
Leave me alone!

Have a helmet hat instead.
A helmet hat protects your head.

Can't you hear me?
NO! I said.

Astronauts wear hats in space.

Jockeys wear them in a race.

This one I know
will look just right.

**I think we're going
to have a fight.**

Oh, no.
Don't fight.
I'll stop.
I will.
Come on.
We'll sit up on the hill.

Do you mean it?

Yes. I do.
I will not mention
hats to you.

Oh, look.
Just look!
Your feet are bare.
I have some shoes
that you can wear.
I'll give you some.
Come over here.

Excuse me while I disappear.